WHIFF

Based on *The Railway Series* by the Rev. W. Awdry

Illustrations by

Robin Davies and Jerry Smith

EGMONT

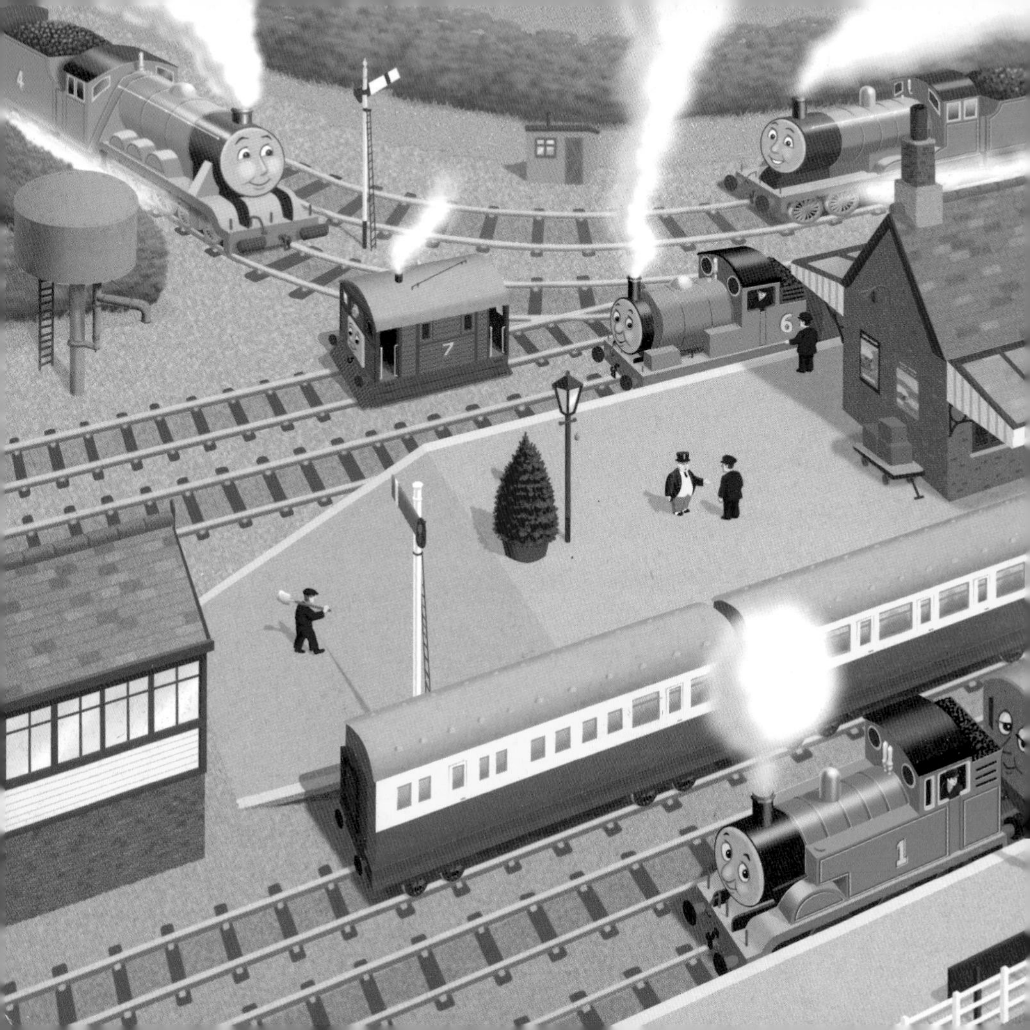

3
5
Annie

EGMONT

We bring stories to life

First published in Great Britain 2008
by Egmont UK Limited
239 Kensington High Street, London W8 6SA

Thomas the Tank Engine & Friends™

CREATED BY BRITT ALLCROFT

Based on the Railway Series by the Reverend W Awdry

HIT entertainment

ISBN 978 1 4052 3786 4
1 3 5 7 9 10 8 6 4 2
Printed in Italy

This is a story about Whiff, a very friendly engine. When he first arrived, I told Emily to work with him. Emily thought that Whiff was scruffy, but she soon saw that it was his kindly ways that really mattered . . .

One morning, Emily was very excited. The Fat Controller had told her to work with a new engine.

"I hope he is smart and useful," she wheeshed.

Emily chuffed away as fast as her boiler could bubble. She steamed into the Shunting Yards to look for the new engine.

The new engine was the scruffiest she had ever seen!

"Hello, Emily," wheeshed the new engine, happily. "My name's Whiff, because people say I'm a bit smelly. You're going to help me collect some rubbish!"

Emily was horrified.

"Come on then," she sighed. "Let's get started."

They soon passed Gordon, James and Henry.

"Hello," whistled Whiff.

"Who's your messy new friend with the funny-sounding whistle, Emily?" snorted James.

"We smelled you coming for miles," wheeshed Gordon, grandly.

"My name's Whiff," whistled Whiff.

"It suits you," laughed Henry. "Phew!"

Emily was very embarrassed. She hurried away, with Whiff puffing after her.

Up the line, Emily and Whiff passed more engines. When they saw Whiff, they all laughed. Emily was tired of being teased.

"I must get away from Whiff," she huffed.

Emily pumped her pistons.

"Wait for me!" whistled Whiff.

But Emily wasn't going to wait for Whiff, and speeded up instead. Soon, Whiff was a long way behind. Emily was glad he was gone.

Later, Emily saw Elizabeth at a crossing.

"Where's the new engine?" honked Elizabeth.

"Er … he got lost," wheeshed Emily.

"No I didn't," whistled Whiff, happily. "Hello!"

"Oh," sniffed Elizabeth. "Aren't you going to introduce me to your new friend?"

But Emily didn't want anything more to do with Whiff. She chuffed away as fast as her pistons could pump.

"Wait for me!" whistled Whiff, cheerfully.

Up ahead, Emily saw a branch line. "Maybe if I puff down here, Whiff won't see me."

Emily chuffed all around The Fat Controller's railway, trying to hide from Whiff. But everywhere that Emily went, Whiff always found her, in every tunnel and in every siding!

Until, at last, she managed to escape from the scruffy little engine.

"Thank goodness," Emily wheeshed. "Now no one will laugh at me for working with such a dirty engine."

Up ahead, Emily saw a very cross Spencer.

"I'm meant to be taking the Duke and Duchess of Boxford to an important lunch!" he huffed. "But my way is blocked by all these smelly rubbish trucks!"

"Flatten my funnel!" steamed Emily.

Emily and Whiff should have cleared the trucks earlier.

Emily knew it was her job to move the rubbish trucks. She buffered up and pushed as hard as she could, but the trucks were much too heavy for her to move on her own.

Just then, Gordon and James chuffed past.

"Can you help me move these rubbish trucks?" tooted Emily.

"Me?" snorted Gordon. "Certainly not!"

"Ugh! No, thank you," wheeshed James.

Emily was upset.

“I’m still waiting!” huffed Spencer.

“If Whiff were here now, he’d be happy to help me,” Emily sighed. “He wanted to be my friend but I was unkind to him. I must find Whiff and say sorry!”

Emily looked high and low for Whiff, but he was nowhere to be seen.

Then, at last, she heard Whiff's funny whistle.

"Hello, Emily," whistled Whiff, cheerfully. "I wondered where you'd got to."

"I'm sorry I ran away from you," puffed Emily.

"That's all right," whistled Whiff. "I'm just glad you found me again. Let's get to work!"

Spencer was getting very impatient.

"Don't worry, Spencer," tooted Emily. "Whiff is here to help now."

"Freeze my firebox!" snorted Spencer, when he saw Whiff. "That scruffy engine can't move all these rubbish trucks!"

"We're going to move them together," chuffed Emily, proudly.

"Oh, thank you Emily!" whistled Whiff.

SPENCER

Spencer watched as Emily and Whiff coupled up to the rubbish trucks and quickly shunted them away.

Spencer was very impressed. "Whiff is a very, very useful engine!" he wheeshed.

"I know," bubbled Emily, happily. "And he's my new, good friend too!"

4
7
6
1

3
5

The Thomas Story Library is THE definitive collection of stories about Thomas and ALL his friends.

5 more Thomas Story Library titles will be chuffing into your local bookshop in 2009!

Stanley

Flora

Colin

Hank

Madge

And there are even more Thomas Story Library books to follow lat

So go on, add to your Thomas Story Library NOW!

A Fantastic Offer for Thomas the Tank Engine Fans!

In every Thomas Story Library book like this one, you will find a special token. Collect 6 Thomas tokens and we will send you a brilliant Thomas poster, and a double-sided bedroom door hanger! Simply tape a £1 coin in the space above, and fill out the form overleaf.

TO BE COMPLETED BY AN ADULT

To apply for this great offer, ask an adult to complete the coupon below and send it with a pound coin and 6 tokens, to:
THOMAS OFFERS, PO BOX 715, HORSHAM RH12 5WG

☐ Please send a Thomas poster and door hanger. I enclose 6 tokens plus a £1 coin. (Price includes P&P)

Fan's name..

Address...

....Postcode.............................

Date of birth...

Name of parent/guardian...

Signature of parent/guardian..

Please allow 28 days for delivery. Offer is only available while stocks last. We reserve the right to change the terms of this offer at any time and we offer a 14 day money back guarantee. This does not affect your statutory rights.

☐ Data Protection Act: If you do not wish to receive other similar offers from us or companies we recommend, please tick this box. Offers apply to UK only.